Teapot and the Dragon

WRITTEN & ILLUSTRATED BY

Nick Jordan

Published by
Clink Street Publishing
2015

ISBN: 978-1-909477-69-8
Ebook: 978-1-909477-70-4

for Juliet
and you

Not so far away, on the other side of teatime,
lie a little group of islands.

Prince Spoon, of Cup and Saucer, and Lord Lid
of Lid, both want to marry Princess Rosehip,
the King and Queen of Teapot's only daughter.

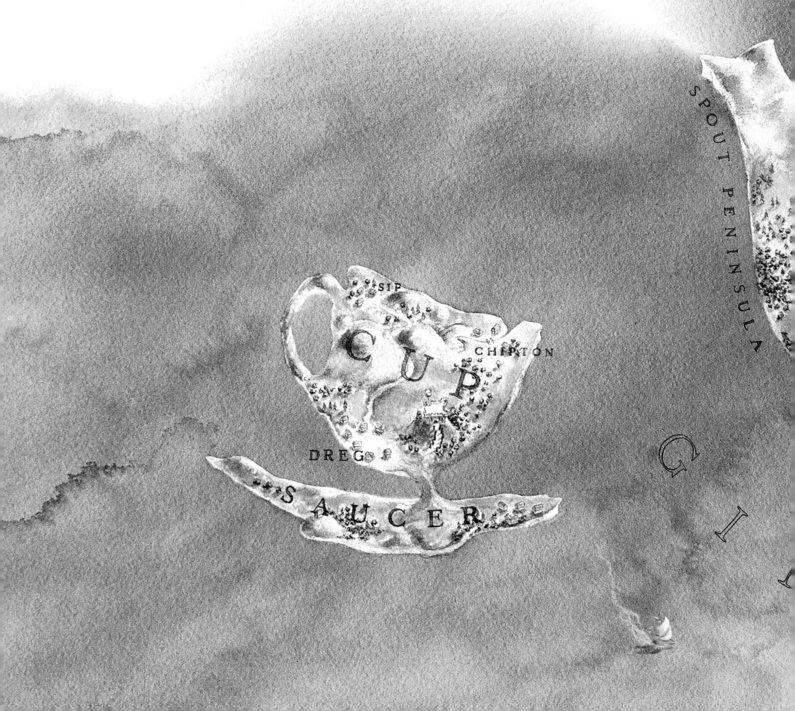

Sunk in soft pillows, in her big comfy bed, Princess Rosehip lay... wide-awake.

'Orrh!' she thought, 'being a princess is sooo boring.'

'How exciting your hyacinth,' cooed Nanny Cosy cheerfully, as she came in to tidy. 'Just think! Prince Spoon and Lord Lid of Lid are coming to Teapot today to find out which of them you are going to marry.'

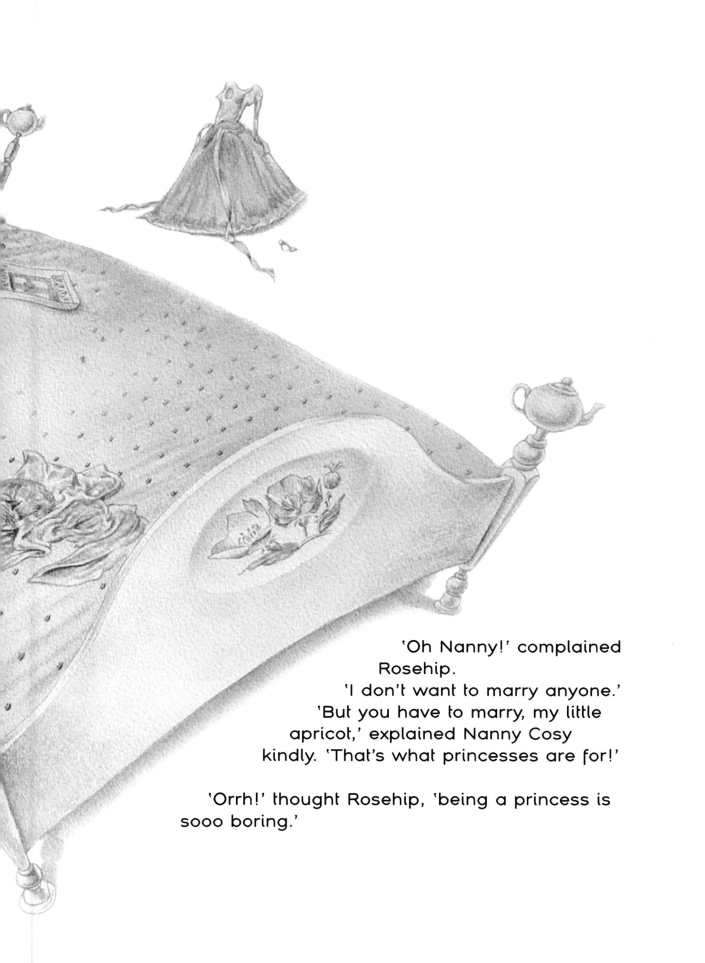

'Oh Nanny!' complained
Rosehip.
'I don't want to marry anyone.'
'But you have to marry, my little
apricot,' explained Nanny Cosy
kindly. 'That's what princesses are for!'

'Orrh!' thought Rosehip, 'being a princess is
sooo boring.'

Blaring trumpets filled the great hall
with a musical din as Prince Spoon
and Lord Lid of Lid came in.
'Your majesties,' said Prince Spoon,
'I have sailed from Saucer to claim
your daughter for my bride.'
'A wasted trip,' sneered Lord Lid,
'for I, Lord Lid of Lid, have come
to marry her too.'

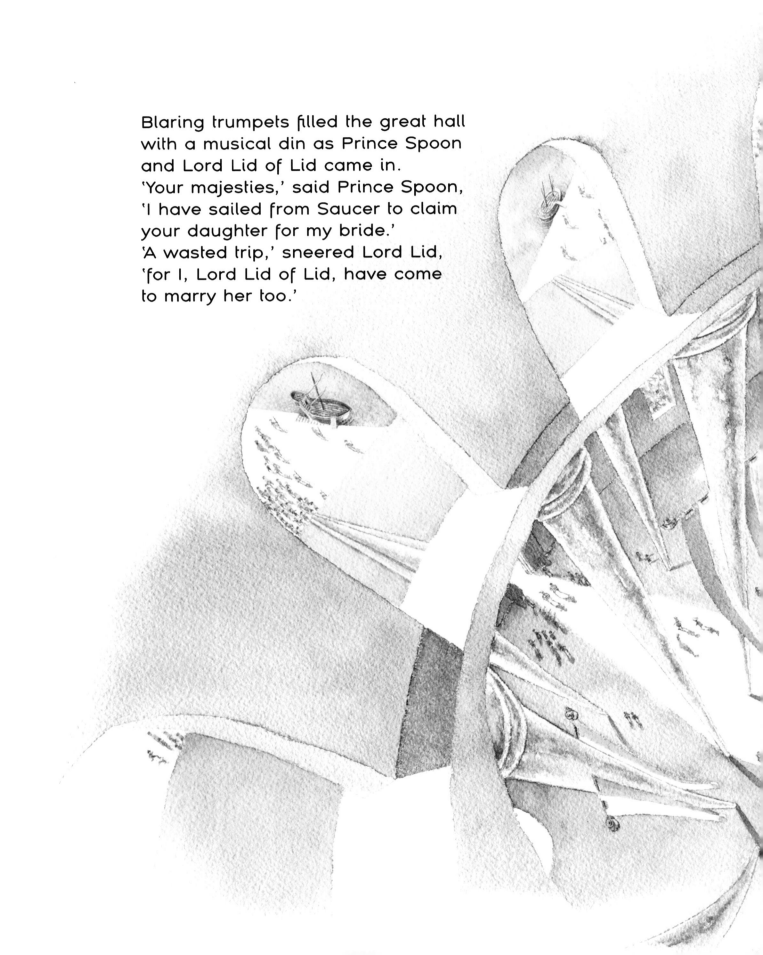

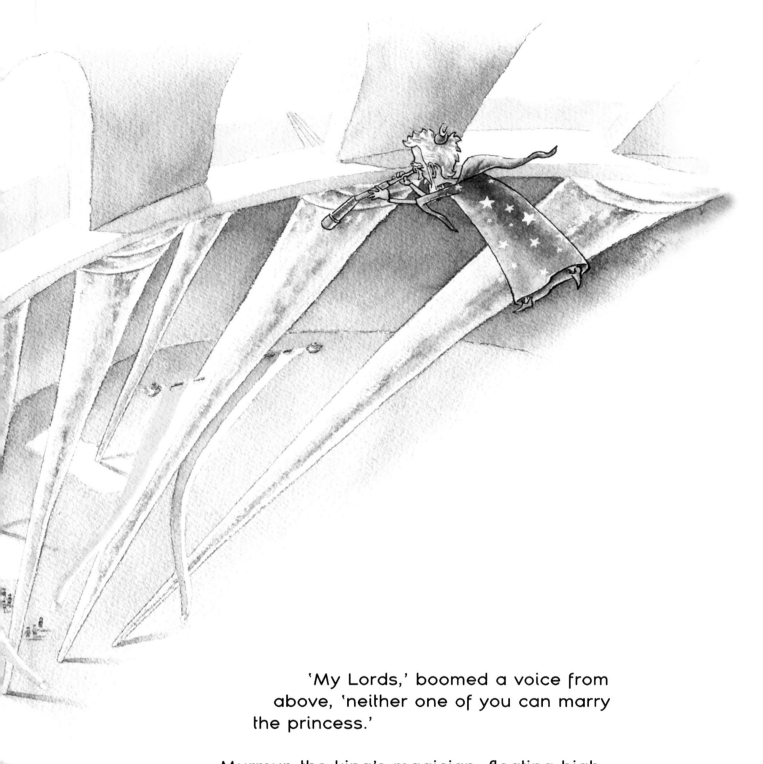

'My Lords,' boomed a voice from
above, 'neither one of you can marry
the princess.'

Murmur, the king's magician, floating high
above, glided down to explain.
'Through my magic telescope,' he said, as he
gently hovered overhead, 'I have seen a fearsome,
fire-breathing beastie, a huge and hungry dragon!'

With a flick-flack of his telescope a massive map of Teapot, and the other islands, unfolded and floated in front of them. 'This dreadful dragon,' said Murmur, 'has made its nest here.' And, as he pointed, a loud

'BOOFOOM!'

made everyone jump, as smoke poured from the tip of Spout Peninsula.

A shocked gasp passed round the great hall.

To stop this beastie,' continued Murmur, 'we must feed it some of its favourite food, and dragons smack their lips for large helpings of...' Murmur paused '...princess and chips!'

'Ooooh!' groaned the Queen, as both she and the King fainted to the floor.

Just then Princess Rosehip came in.

As both Lid and Spoon rushed to greet her, they
tripped over the King and, grabbing the nearest
thing to stop them falling, pulled Sir Teabag on
top of them!

Murmur took Rosehip aside and explained
how dragons liked princesses... a lot!
'Well,' thought Rosehip, 'at least meeting
a dragon won't be boring.'

'I, brave Prince Spoon,' said brave Prince Spoon, as he climbed out from under Teabag and Lid, '...shall go with you Princess. With a quick swish swash of my silver sword, I shall kill this beastly dragon.'

Sir Teabag turned to see if Lord Lid was going to leap up and offer to go too, but Lord Lid had left.

He was already sailing back to Lid!

With bags packed and a much smaller map, they set off for Spout with Spoon's servant, Onelump, carrying the royal luggage.

'Thank goodness Prince Spoon and his silver sword are coming too,' thought Rosehip.
'I just hope he's as brave as he says he is.'
For she found the thought of being crunched by a dragon's huge, pointy teeth really very scary!

As Spout got nearer and nearer, so Rosehip's fear grew and grew, until she thought she saw dragons leaping out at her everywhere!

Prince Spoon didn't see any dragons.
'I don't see any dragons,' he said. But he spoke
too soon, for just then a loud dragony
voice roared…

'Me's a big huge Dragon!
me's fierce and angry
me tummy's rumbling
coz me's jolly hungry!
Me snapping jaws,
and me smacking lips
is impatient for me portion
of princess and chips!'

Then everything went black!

Spoon woke to find Onelump next to him,
quietly dripping. They were both wet, but why?
It was a bright blue sunny day.
Turning round they saw a huge watering can
and attached to the watering can was a great
big huge… DRAGON!!

Spoon and Onelump ran and ran and didn't
stop until they got back to the palace at
Pot Bottom.

The King and Queen, seeing that Rosehip
wasn't with them, both flopped flat in another
faint!

Sir Teabag ordered a royal bucket of water
to wake them, while Murmur organised
a rescue party.

'Let us hope we are not too late,' mumbled
Murmur as they all ran to the rescue, with the
King and Queen squelching behind in soggy
socks and shoes.

At last they arrived at the dragon's lair and
found the fierce and frightening beast...
sitting in the middle of a vegetable patch.
It didn't move. No one moved.

Then, suddenly, the dragon... snored!

'It's asleep,' murmured Murmur.
'But it's sitting down,' said Sir Teabag.
'Dragon's always sleep sitting down,'
said Murmur. 'If they slept lying
down they would crease their wings.'

Prince Spoon, with sword drawn,
bravely tiptoed toward the snoring
monster....

As Spoon wasn't tall enough, he climbed on top of the others.

But now he was too tall! So he started to climb down again.

The King wobbled, Onelump wobbled, Sir Teabag wobbled and 'WHACK!' as they all tumbled to the ground, Spoon's sword thwacked the dragon on its nose.

'OW!' said the dragon. 'Oops!' said Spoon.

'Aha!' cried Murmur as he turned a page in a book he had brought. 'This dragon hasn't eaten the princess.' 'How do you know?' asked the King. 'It says here it only eats vegetables,' explained Murmur.

'**SHE** only eats vegetables,'
corrected the dragon.
'You can talk!' exclaimed the Queen.
'Of course I can talk.'
'You're a girl!' said Prince Spoon.
'Of course I'm a girl.'

'But if this dragon...' began the King,
'Oh do call me Jenny'.

'If err, Jenny...' continued the King,
'if Jenny didn't eat our daughter,
who did?'

'Have you asked the other
dragon?' suggested Jenny
helpfully.

It was still dark when Rosehip awoke. A single candle flickered against blotchy red walls.

'So,' she thought, 'this is what it's like inside a dragon's tummy.'

Rosehip was beginning to think that being inside a dragon's tummy was almost as boring as being stuck in the palace with nothing to do, when suddenly a door in the dragon's tummy wall opened and in walked...

Lord Lid!

'What rotten luck,' thought Rosehip. 'Lid's the last person I wanted to be eaten with.'

'Ha ha my princess,' said Lid, 'now we can be married.'

'I'm sorry,' replied the princess, 'but I'm not going to marry you just because we are mouthfuls of the same meal.'

'No no my princess,' replied Lord Lid, as he pulled back a red curtain. 'We have not been eaten by the dragon!'

'See, I AM THE DRAGON!' he said, showing off his dragon costume with a crafty smile. 'I knocked Spoon out and brought you here to Castle Lid. Now you are my prisoner, and we shall be married.'

'Now that really is boring,' thought Rosehip.

'ANOTHER DRAGON!' cried
the king, as he and the Queen fainted again.

'Would you recognise this other dragon?'
asked Murmur.

'Of course,' said Jenny. And she flicked
through Murmur's book of dragons until
she found the page...

'There he is,' she said. 'I recognise that funny red nose and saggy sackcloth skin.'

Dragonium Impostersaurus Vex:
an evil little man pretending to be a
dragon. Badly dressed up and
up to no good!

'Why I recognise this dragon,'
said Murmur.
'It's Lord Lid of Lid in disguise!'

'Please?' asked Lid for the twenty-ninth time.
'No,' replied Rosehip
'Oh, pleeeease marry me?'
'NO!'

Just then there was a whooshing sound
followed by a loud Kerplonk! Whooosh...
Kerplonk! There it goes again, and again.

One of Lid's guards, called Gunpowder,
rushed in. 'My Lord, the castle is being
attacked. It's raining cabbages!'

'Ha!' thought Lid, 'in my dragon costume
I'll soon scare away whoever dares throw
cabbages at me.'

Locking the princess in the castle, he jumped
into his boat and ordered Gunpowder to row
them both across to Teapot.

Bonk whooosh...kerplonk! Jenny kicked
another cabbage at Castle Lid.

Through his telescope Murmur spied Lid's boat.
'Cease-fire!' he called. Stopping suddenly, in
mid-kick, Jenny lost her balance and fell
backwards in a cloud of dust with a great

KAₐBLUMPHH!

'Growl growl roar roar!' snarled Lid as his boat bumped against the shore. 'Me's a big huge dragon and me's jolly fierce and very hungry so you'd better run for your lives!' he advised.

'No,' said Prince Spoon calmly, as he drew his silver sword, 'I think I'll stay and fight you actually.'
'But I'm a Dragon!' said Lid. 'I really think you ought to run away.'

'No,' said Spoon. 'I think I'll stay. After all I have Jenny on my side.'

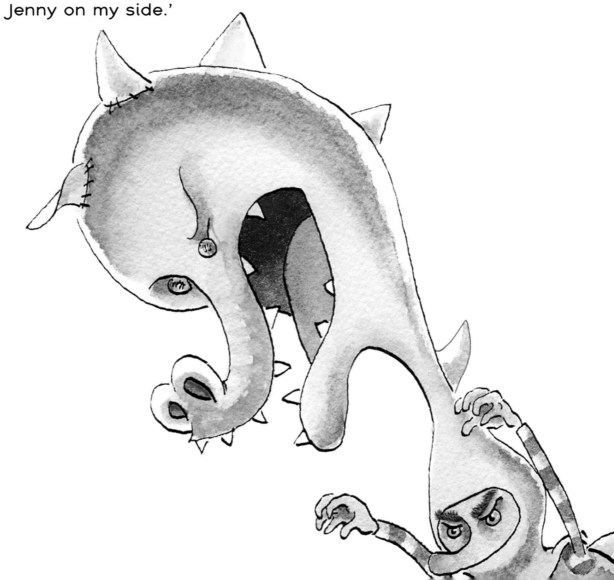

'Jenny who...?'
'How do you do?' said Jenny as she got up
and dusted herself down.
'AAAAH! A real dragon!' screamed Lid.
'Help Mummy!' he cried, and he fell out of
his boat in surprise.

With a Flop SPLOOSH! Lid landed in the sea
and as his dragon costume filled with water
he began to sink, rather quickly actually.
'Gurgle gurgle!' he gurgled, 'I can't swim!'

Spoon sighed and, passing his sword and cloak to Jenny for safe keeping, he dived in to rescue the sinking Lord Lid of Lid.

Lid was so glad to get back on dry land he passed the castle key to Gunpowder and ordered him to row back to Lid and collect the princess.

The King and Queen, seeing their darling daughter safe, and still in one piece, fainted again! But this time, with happiness.

Rosehip nearly fainted too when she saw Jenny's big pointy teeth and claws.

But it wasn't long before she realised that real dragons are never as scary as the dragons we imagine.

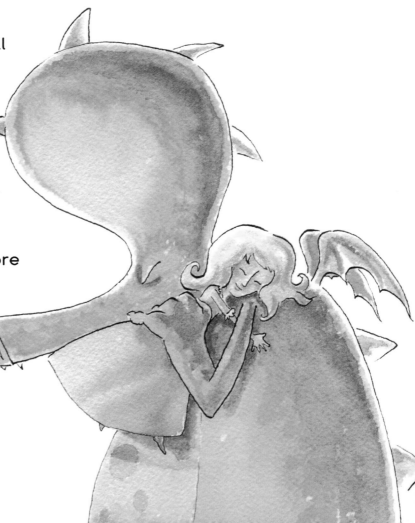

'Darling Rosehip,' said Prince Spoon, as he
sank to one knee, 'will you be my princess?'
'But I'm already a princess,' replied Rosehip.

Murmur whispered in Rosehip's ear,
'the prince is asking you to marry him
your highness.'

'Oh!' said Rosehip.

It was then that Rosehip realised she loved Prince Spoon because he was brave and wasn't boring.

Everyone had a lovely time at the royal wedding, and Princess Rosehip had the biggest bridesmaid ever!

So everyone on Teapot lived happily ever after. Or at least until... but that's another story.

the end